A Happy Hat

Copyright © 2014 by Magination Press, an imprint of the American Psychological Association.
Originally published in Korean language as *A Happy Hat* copyright © EenBook Co., 2011.
All rights reserved. Except as permitted under the United States Copyright Act of 1976, no part
of this publication may be reproduced or distributed in any form or by any means, or stored
in a database or retrieval system, without the prior written permission of the publisher.

Published by

MAGINATION PRESS
An Educational Publishing Foundation Book
American Psychological Association
750 First Street NE
Washington, DC 20002

For more information about our books, including a complete catalog,
please write to us, call 1-800-374-2721, or visit our website at www.apa.org/pubs/magination.

Printed by Worzalla, Stevens Point, WI

Library of Congress Cataloging-in-Publication Data

Kim, Cecil.
A happy hat / by Cecil Kim ; illustrated by Joo-Kyung Kim. — English edition.
pages cm
"Originally published in Korean language as A Happy Hat copyright (c) EenBook Co., 2011."
"An Educational Publishing Foundation Book."
Summary: A hat recalls how it was first worn by a happy groom at his wedding, then passed
through many hands over the years, wondering what each change would bring but finding
pleasure in all.
ISBN-13: 978-1-4338-1337-5 (hardcover)
ISBN-10: 1-4338-1337-8 (hardcover)
ISBN-13: 978-1-4338-1338-2 (pbk.)
ISBN-10: 1-4338-1338-6 (pbk.)
[1. Resilience (Personality trait)–Fiction. 2. Contentment–Fiction. 3. Hats–Fiction.]
I. Kim, Joo-Kyung, illustrator. II. Title.
PZ7.K55958Hap 2014
[E]–dc23   2013004772

A Happy Hat

by Cecil Kim

illustrated by Joo-Kyung Kim

MAGINATION PRESS • WASHINGTON, DC
American Psychological Association

This English edition is published by arrangement with EenBook Co., through the ChoiceMaker Korea Co.

I am a hat.

I am worn out here and there. I have a few holes, and even a few weeds sticking out.

But I am still very much a hat. A very happy hat.

I have lots of stories to tell.

A long time ago, the most popular hat maker in the city made me,

a shiny black silk hat decorated with peacock feathers.

Lots of fashionable gentlemen wanted a hat like me.

My first owner was a new groom with many dreams. I fit wonderfully on his head.

His wedding was held on a dazzling spring day.

The bride wore a beautiful white dress.

The air was filled with the sounds of guests clapping and laughing.

Every minute of that day was full of hope and good wishes, like a flower starting to blossom.

I felt glad and content, filled with hope.

I felt special.

After some time, I went to a second-hand store for sale.

I wondered if I was too old.

I wondered if I was not interesting anymore.

I wondered if I was of no use to anyone.

But I am a hat.

A little worn with a hole or two, but still, I am a hat.

A special hat.

My next owner was a magician.

He pulled pigeons from me,
made roses bloom and snowflakes fall.

Children kept their bright eyes focused on me,
holding their breath.

Dogs sniffed the air for clues.
Parents winked knowingly.

I felt lucky and alive, full of curiosity.

I felt wonderful.

Time went on. I was sold
to a street musician.

I sat upside down on the
cold pavement.

People threw coins into me
as the musician played violin.

Cats meowed. Children danced
and giggled all around me.

The coins I held fed the
musician's hungry family.

I felt helpful and wonderful,
filled with generosity.

I felt joyful.

Then one day... *Woof! Woof!*

A stray dog grabbed me and took off running.

I wondered where he was taking me.

I wondered what would happen next.

I wondered if I would be lost forever.

That is how I ended up
in these woods.

I was alone in the woods.

I wondered what I would do next.

I wondered when I would become someone's hat again.

But whenever I felt lonely or confused, I remembered:

When the rain and wind pass, I might see a rainbow.

When night is over, I will see the sun rise.

When winter is over, spring will arrive.

WHOOSH!

I heard the flapping of wings.

Someone, something was approaching!

A mother bird settled on my brim.

All day long, she brought grass, soil,
and cotton in her mouth to build a nest inside me.

Her devotion.

Her warmth.

Her love.

I felt like a treasure, filled with happiness.

I felt valuable.

Now I am waiting for my next owner.

Will it be one, two, or three baby birds?

Their mother's love overflows in me.

I am filled with wonder, generosity, and courage.

I am the happiest hat in the world!

The hat was left in the woods. What is the hat thinking?

 What are the magician and street musician thinking?

After the baby birds leave, who will become the Happy Hat's next owner?

Draw a picture of who it might be.

Note to Parents and Other Caregivers

by Mary Lamia, PhD

Getting through tough times and rough patches in life has much to do with resilience and optimism—the capacity to recover from adversity and to have hope. Children can be taught how to handle disappointments and figure out what to do when an expectation or goal is blocked. These skills buffer their psychological well-being and help them to bounce back after stressful events.

Resilient and hopeful children handle disappointment differently than those who are not as resilient. Resilient children do not dwell on present unpleasant circumstances, but rather remain hopeful that future experiences can be positive. Not only can this attitude buffer against stress, it can reduce the impact of negative events or dissatisfaction. The positive feelings a child experiences as she looks ahead, imagining hopefully what might happen, what she will attain, or who she is going to be, can influence how she currently views herself. Along with hope comes her prediction that she will be happy, and this can ameliorate the current dissatisfaction or disappointment.

Being optimistic about the future helps a child recognize that he is adaptable and capable, and therefore able to get through a tough time. Those children who are hopeful and optimistic do not dwell on negative outcomes, while those who are pessimistic may become resentful or negatively preoccupied. Nevertheless, optimism alone does not always guide a child in the right direction. When an obstacle or stressful life experience presents itself, helping a child learn to recognize and name the emotions he is experiencing at the time, and encouraging him to realistically consider a new course of action by presenting him with options to consider, will develop his resilience, problem-solving, and self-confidence.

Optimistic or resilient children are not just born; resilience and optimism can be learned and developed. A strong bond with a loving and trusted caregiver positively influences a child's ability to respond to difficulty, hardship, and distress. Resilience may also develop as a result of identifying with adults who model optimistic and resilient responses to adversity and stress. In addition, there are other things that a parent or caregiver can do. The American Psychological Association suggests ten ways to build resilience in children and teens. These include:

- **Make connections.** Teach your child how to make friends, including the skill of empathy, or feeling another's pain. Encourage your child to be a friend in order to get friends. Build a strong family network to support your child through his or her inevitable disappointments and hurts. At school, watch to make sure that one child is not being isolated. Connecting with people provides social support and strengthens resilience. Some find comfort in connecting with a higher power, whether through organized religion or privately, and you may wish to introduce your child to your own traditions of worship.

- **Help your child by having him or her help others.** Children who may feel helpless can be empowered by helping others. Engage your child in age-appropriate volunteer work, or ask for assistance yourself with some task that he or she can master. At school, brainstorm with children about ways they can help others.

- **Maintain a daily routine.** Sticking to a routine can be comforting to children, especially younger children who crave structure in their lives. Encourage your child to develop his or her own routines.

- **Take a break.** While it is important to stick to routines, endlessly worrying can be counter-productive. Teach your child how to focus on something besides what's worrying him. Be aware of what your child is exposed to that can be troubling, whether it be news, the Internet, or overheard conversations, and make sure your child takes a break from those things if they trouble her. Although schools are being held accountable for performance on standardized tests, build in unstructured time during the school day to allow children to be creative.

- **Teach your child self-care.** Make yourself a good example, and teach your child the importance of making time to eat properly, exercise and rest. Make sure your child has time to have fun, and make sure that your child hasn't scheduled every moment of his or her life with no "down time" to relax. Caring for oneself and even having fun will help your child stay balanced and better deal with stressful times.

- **Move toward your goals.** Teach your child to set reasonable goals and then to move toward them one step at a time. Moving toward that goal—even if it's a tiny step—and receiving praise for doing so will focus your child on what he or she has accomplished rather than on what hasn't been accomplished, and can help build the resilience to move forward in the face of challenges. At school, break down large assignments into small, achievable goals for younger children, and for older children, acknowledge accomplishments on the way to larger goals.

- **Nurture a positive self-view.** Help your child remember ways that he or she has successfully handled hardships in the past and then help him understand that these past challenges help him build the strength to handle future challenges. Help your child learn to trust himself to solve problems and make appropriate decisions. Teach your child to see the humor in life, and the ability to laugh at oneself. At school, help children see how their individual accomplishments contribute to the well-being of the class as a whole.

- **Keep things in perspective and maintain a hopeful outlook.** Even when your child is facing very painful events, help him look at the situation in a broader context and keep a long-term perspective. Although your child may be too young to consider a long-term look on his own, help him or her see that there is a future beyond the current situation and that the future can be good. An optimistic and positive outlook enables your child to see the good things in life and keep going even in the hardest times. In school, use history to show that life moves on after bad events.

- **Look for opportunities for self-discovery.** Tough times are often the times when children learn the most about themselves. Help your child take a look at how whatever he is facing can teach him "what he is made of." At school, consider leading discussions of what each student has learned after facing down a tough situation.

- **Accept that change is part of living.** Change often can be scary for children and teens. Help your child see that change is part of life and new goals can replace goals that have become unattainable. In school, point out how students have changed as they moved up in grade levels and discuss how that change has had an impact on the students.*

Parents can do much to build resilience in their child. It may be worthwhile to direct your child to reflect upon her endeavors or simply go over her to-do list before bedtime, since the human brain is sensitive to conscious perception of future events and will unconsciously work toward one's goals. When she wakes up in the morning, take a few minutes with her to consider the results of her reflection. However, if your child's difficulties persist, or if she seems to be in particular emotional distress, it may be helpful to seek consultation from a licensed psychologist or psychotherapist.

Mary Lamia, PhD, is a clinical psychologist in Marin County, CA and the author of the Magination Press books *Understanding Myself: A Kid's Guide to Intense Feelings and Strong Emotions* and *Emotions! Making Sense of Your Feelings.*

*From the American Psychological Association's "Resilience Guide for Parents & Teachers" at http://www.apa.org/helpcenter/resilience.aspx.

About the Author

Cecil Kim studied child psychology in her undergraduate and post-graduate studies. She has worked in psychological treatment for children and is currently reaching out to more children and their hopes and dreams through picture books. Her other works include *Crybaby Cloud; Embarrassment, Go Away;* and *Let's Wash Hands First*.

About the Illustrator

Joo-Kyung Kim studied design at university and is now working as a children's book illustrator. She was a runner-up in the 15th and 16th Noma International Concours for Picture Book Illustration. Kim continues to work hard writing and illustrating so that children can enjoy more fun and entertaining stories. Among her other published works are *Red Goblin, Tell Me About Cells; Star Family Takes Off on a Journey of the Solar System;* and *The Three Musketeers of Goguryo Pyungyang-Sung*.

About Magination Press

Magination Press is an imprint of the American Psychological Association, the largest scientific and professional organization representing psychologists in the United States and the largest association of psychologists worldwide.